MR. JELLY

by Roger Hargreaves

Poor Mr Jelly was frightened of everything and anything.

At the slightest little thing he would quiver and tremble and shake and turn to jelly.

So, it's not really surprising to find that Mr Jelly lives as far away from anybody that he can find.

In the middle of a wood, miles and miles from anywhere.

This story begins one morning when Mr Jelly was asleep.

It was a beautiful autumn morning. The sun was shining. The leaves on the trees had turned to a glorious red. And the wind stirred gently in the treetops.

A single leaf fell gently from the tree right outside Mr Jelly's house and quietly brushed against his bedroom window as it fell.

Mr Jelly awoke with a start.

"What's that terrible noise?" he cried. "Oh heavens! The house is falling down! Oh disaster! It's an earthquake! Oh calamity! It's the end of the world!"

And he hid under the bedclothes, trembling with fright.

After an hour, by which time he realised that his house wasn't falling down, and there wasn't an earthquake, and the world wasn't coming to an end, Mr Jelly peeped out from under the bedclothes.

"Phew," he said. "Thank goodness for that!"

And he got up and went downstairs to make his breakfast.

Mr Jelly poured some cornflakes out of a packet on to a plate.

Then he poured some milk on to the cornflakes.

Then he went to the cupboard to get some sugar.

Snap! Crackle! Pop! went the cornflakes in the milk.

"Oh goodness gracious!" cried Mr Jelly, diving under the kitchen table. "Oh dear! I hear guns! Oh calamity! It's war!"

But of course it wasn't.

And of course Mr Jelly eventually came out from under the table and ate up all his cornflakes.

After breakfast Mr Jelly thought that he'd go for a walk.

He was walking through the woods which surround his house when a worm poked his head out of the ground.

"Morning," said the worm cheerfully to Mr Jelly.

Mr Jelly nearly jumped out of his skin.

"What?" he shouted. "Who's there?" And then he saw the worm. "Oh good heavens! It's a snake! Oh dear! A man-eating snake! Oh calamity! I'm going to be eaten alive!" And he jumped up into a tree.

"What a performance," commented the worm, and went back into his hole.

After an hour Mr Jelly felt brave enough to climb down from the tree and continue his walk.

Eventually he came out of the other side of the wood and into a field.

Mr Jelly glanced nervously around.

It was an empty field.

Or was it?

In the long grass in the middle of the field, unseen by Mr Jelly, there was a tramp enjoying a sleep in the autumn sunshine.

Mr Jelly picked his way cautiously through the grass.

The tramp, fast asleep, snored.

"What was that?" shrieked Mr Jelly. "It's a lion!
I heard it growl! Oh goodness gracious! Oh dear
me! A lion! A huge lion! A huge lion with enormous
teeth! A huge lion with sharp teeth that's going to
bite me in two! A huge ferocious lion with
enormous sharp teeth that's going to bite me in two,
if not three!"

And he fainted.

All this commotion awakened the tramp, who yawned, stretched, sat up and saw Mr Jelly lying on the ground beside him.

"Oh dear," he said, for he was a kindly tramp. "Oh dear." And he picked up Mr Jelly and placed him gently in the palm of his hand.

Mr Jelly came to, and sat up rubbing his eyes.

Then he saw the tramp's face looking at him.

"Oh disaster!" he screamed. "Oh calamity! It's a giant! An ogre! Oh gracious! He's going to have me for breakfast!"

"My, my," said the tramp gently. "You're a nervous little chap, aren't you? What's your name?"

"Mr J . . . J . . . J . . . J . . . J . . . J . . . Jelly," stammered Mr Jelly.

"I used to be nervous like you," said the tramp, "but I learned how not to be! Would you like me to tell you the secret?"

Mr Jelly quivered and shook and said, "YYY . Y . . . Yes. P . . . P . . . P . . . Please."

"It's very simple," continued the tramp. "All you have to do is count up to ten, and you'll find that whatever's frightening you isn't quite so frightening after all!"

Then he set Mr Jelly gently down on the grass.

"Remember," he said to Mr Jelly. "Count to ten!" And off he went.

Mr Jelly thought that it would be a very good idea if he went home immediately.

Back across the field he went.

Back through the woods he went.

He was walking through the woods when he stepped on a little twig.

Snap! went the twig.

Mr Jelly jumped twice his own height in terror.

"What was that?" he shrieked. "That terrible snapping noise? It's a tree falling down that's going to crush me to pieces! Oh calamity! It's a crocodile hiding in the bushes snapping its teeth! Oh disaster! It's . . ." And then he stopped.

He took a deep breath.

"Onetwothreefourfivesixseveneightnineten!" he said.

And saw that what had gone snap was a twig. A silly old twig.

"Phew!" he said.

Mr Jelly had almost reached his house when a leaf drifted gently down from a tree, on top of him.

"Help! Police! Murder!" he screamed. "I'm being kidnapped! Oh calamity! It's ruffians! With guns! They're going to . . ." And then he stopped.

He took a deep breath.

"Onetwothreefourfivesixseveneightnineten!"

And then he saw what had fallen on him was only a leaf.

Nothing but a leaf!

A stupid red leaf!

"It works," he said out loud in wonderment.

And do you know, it did work.

After that moment, Mr Jelly became a changed man.

Well, you can see that by looking at him, can't you?

And he never shrieks, or shouts, or screams, or quivers, or shakes, or trembles any more.

And he never hides under the bedclothes any more.

Well.

Not very often, anyway!

3 Great Offers For Mr Men Fans

1 FREE Door Hangers and Posters

In every Mr Men and Little Miss Book like this one you will find a special token. Collect 6 and we will send you either a brilliant Mr. Men or Little Miss poster and a Mr Men or Little Miss double sided, full colour, bedroom door hanger. Apply using the coupon overleaf, enclosing six tokens and a 50p coin for your choice of two items.

Egmont World tokens can be used towards any other Egmont World / World International token scheme promotions, in early learning and story / activity books.

Posters: Tick your preferred choice of either Mr Men ☐ or Little Miss ☐

Door Hangers: Choose from: Mr. Nosey & Mr Muddle ☐, Mr Greedy & Mr Lazy ☐, Mr Tickle & Mr Grumpy ☐, Mr Slow & Mr Busy ☐ Mr Messy & Mr Quiet ☐, Mr Perfect & Mr Forgetful ☐, Little Miss Fun & Little Miss Late ☐, Little Miss Helpful & Little Miss Tidy ☐, Little Miss Busy & Little Miss Brainy ☐, Little Miss Star & Little Miss Fun ☐. (Please tick)

2 Mr Men Library Boxes

Keep your growing collection of Mr Men and Little Miss books in these superb library boxes. With an integral carrying handle and stay-closed fastener, these full colour, plastic boxes are fantastic. They are just £5.49 each including postage. Order overleaf.

3 Join The Club

To join the fantastic Mr Men & Little Miss Club, check out the page overleaf NOW!

Allow 28 days for delivery. We reserve the right to change the terms of this offer at any time but we offer a 14 day money back guarantee. The money-back guarantee does not affect your statutory rights. Birthday and Christmas cards are sent care of parent/guardians in advance of the day. After 31/12/00 please call to check that the offer details are still correct.

MR MEN and LITTLE MISS™ & © 1998 Mrs. Roger Hargreaves

· RETURN THIS WHOLE PAGE ·

Join Our Club!

MR.MEN & Little Miss CLUB

When you become a member of the fantastic Mr Men and Little Miss Club you'll receive a personal letter from Mr Happy and Little Miss Giggles, a club badge with your name, and a superb Welcome Pack (pictured below right).

You'll also get birthday and Christmas cards from the Mr Men and Little Misses, 2 newsletters crammed with special offers, privileges and news, and a copy of the 12 page Mr Men catalogue which includes great party ideas.

If it were on sale in the shops, the Welcome Pack alone might cost around £13. But a year's membership is just £9.99 (plus 73p postage) with a 14 day money-back guarantee if you are not delighted!

HOW TO APPLY To apply for any of these three great offers, ask an adult to complete the coupon below and send it with appropriate payment and tokens (where required) to: Mr Men Offers, PO Box 7, Manchester M19 2HD. Credit card orders for Club membership ONLY by telephone, please call: 01403 242727.

To be completed by an adult

❏ **1.** Please send a poster and door hanger as selected overleaf. I enclose six tokens and a 50p coin for post (coin not required if you are also taking up 2. or 3. below).

❏ **2.** Please send ___ Mr Men Library case(s) and ___ Little Miss Library case(s) at £5.49 each.

❏ **3.** Please enrol the following in the Mr Men & Little Miss Club at £10.72 (inc postage)

Fan's Name:_____Fan's Address:_____

_____Post Code:_____Date of birth:___/___/___

Your Name:_____Your Address:_____

Post Code:_____Name of parent or guardian (if not you):_____

Total amount due: £_____ (£5.49 per Library Case, £10.72 per Club membership)

❏ I enclose a cheque or postal order payable to Egmont World Limited.

❏ Please charge my MasterCard / Visa account.

Card number: | | | | | | | | | | | | | | | | |

Expiry Date: _____/_____   Signature: _____

Data Protection Act: If you do **not** wish to receive other family offers from us or companies we recommend, please tick this box ❏. Offer applies to UK only